PEAT MOSS and IVY
Meet SANTA CLAWS

A Random House PICTUREBACK®

PEAT MOSS and IVY
Meet SANTA CLAWS

Michael Berenstain

Random House · New York

Library of Congress Cataloging-in-Publication Data:
Berenstain, Michael. Peat Moss and Ivy meet Santa Claws. (A Random House pictureback)
SUMMARY: Two chipmunks, Peat Moss and Ivy, try to make sure that their letters to Santa
Claws are delivered. [1. Chipmunks—Fiction. 2. Christmas—Fiction] I. Title.
PZ7.B44827Pdj 1987 [E] 86-22029 ISBN: 0-394-88872-3

Manufactured in the United States of America 1 2 3 4 5 6 7 8 9 0

It was Christmastime in the chipmunk hole and everyone was very busy.

Momma Chipmunk was getting out the Christmas decorations, Poppa Chipmunk was putting up the Christmas twig, and Peat Moss and Ivy were writing their letters to Santa Claws.

As Momma was taking the decorations out of their boxes, she saw the little wooden Santa Claws that the chipmunks set on their mantel each year.

The real Santa Claws was a jolly old woodchuck who lived up north on Snow Mountain. Every Christmas Eve he loaded his sleigh with toys and brought them to all the good little rabbits and squirrels, muskrats and moles, and, of course, chipmunks.

"What do you want Santa Claws to bring you this year?" asked Momma.

"Some books," said Ivy.

"And some toys," said Peat Moss.

"And *new ice skates!*" they cried together.

"Our old ones are too small for us," explained Ivy.

"Let's go mail our letters now," said Peat Moss. "We want to make sure they reach Snow Mountain on time."

Peat Moss and Ivy sealed their letters, marked them AIRMAIL, and scampered out the front hole.

As Peat Moss and Ivy were dropping their letters in the mailpod, their friend Hickory Gray Squirrel came by. He was on his way to the skating pond.

"Hi!" called Ivy. "Did you send your letter to Santa Claws yet?"

"Nah!" said Hickory. "I don't believe in Santa Claws anymore."

"You don't?" gasped the two chipmunks.

"Nope," said Hickory. "I just tell my mom and pop what I want for Christmas. This year I asked them for new ice skates—my old ones are nearly worn out."

Just then Mr. Muskrat, the mailman, came along to collect the mail.

"See that?" said Hickory. "I'll bet he doesn't really deliver the letters addressed to Santa Claws."

"Doesn't *deliver* them?" Ivy gulped.

"Of course not!" Hickory chuckled. "You don't think he really sends them all the way to Snow Mountain, do you?" And with a laugh he went on his way to the skating pond.

Peat Moss and Ivy began to worry. What if Hickory was right? What if Mr. Muskrat really *didn't* deliver their letters to Santa Claws? How would Santa know what they wanted for Christmas?

They decided to follow Mr. Muskrat to the post office to see for themselves what he did with their letters.

When they reached the post office, they peeked through the doorway. Mr. Muskrat was sorting the mail.

"Which letters are ours?" whispered Ivy.

"Shhh!" said Peat Moss as they sneaked into the room and hid behind some large mailbags.

Mr. Muskrat picked up a pile of letters and headed for the mailbags.

"Uh-oh!" said Peat Moss. "He'll see us! Quick—hide in here!"

They crawled inside one of the mailbags.

Mr. Muskrat dropped the letters into the mailbag—right on top of Peat Moss and Ivy! Then he lifted the sack and swung it across his back.

"Ooof!" he grunted. "What a *load!"*

TO: SANTA CLAWS
SNOW MOUNTAIN

TO: SAN
SNOW

He carried the sack outside, put it onto his mail truck, and drove off.

He drove straight to the Backyard Airport.

Mr. Muskrat took the sack
to the airmail shed and gave
it to Canada, the express goose.
It was her job to deliver
the mail marked AIRMAIL.

Canada took the sack
in her beak and flapped
down the runway,
beating her wings faster
and faster until she
took off.

Peat Moss and Ivy
were airborne!

Away flew Canada—out of the backyard, up over the People House, high above the woods, past the pond, and toward the hills...

on her way to Snow Mountain.

When at last she came to the top of Snow Mountain, Canada swooped down and dropped the sack right into Santa Claws's mail chute.

The sack tumbled down
a long tunnel and landed
with a *thud!* in Santa Claws's
mail room.

Their heads spinning, Peat Moss and Ivy peeked out of the sack.

"Where are we?" wondered Ivy.

But before they had a chance to crawl out, a mailmouse came into the room and put the sack onto a wheelbarrow.

He wheeled it down a dark twisting tunnel until he came to...

Santa Claws's own study!
   Santa and Mrs. Claws were busy reading their mail.
   "Dump it right here, Joe," Santa told the mailmouse without looking up.

The mailmouse emptied the sack onto the floor. Peat Moss and Ivy slid out and landed at Santa Claws's feet.

"Why, bless my spectacles!" he cried. "Peat Moss and Ivy, isn't it?"

"What are you children doing here?" asked Mrs. Claws.

"Santa Claws!" the two chipmunks gasped.

"We just…we just wanted to be sure our letters reached you."

"Well, of course they did," said Santa, taking a couple of letters off their heads. "Here they are! Safe and sound!"

"We were worried," explained Peat Moss, "because our friend Hickory Gray Squirrel said that there *wasn't* any Santa Claws!"

"He *did?*" said Santa as he opened their letters. "Well, he must be wrong! Look!" he cried, patting his stomach. "Here I am. Ho ho ho!"

"Claws," said Mrs. Claws. "Perhaps Peat Moss and Ivy would like to visit the workshop."

"Why, that's a wonderful idea!" Santa said, pulling out his watch. "It *is* time for me to make my rounds."

"Oh, yes!" said Peat Moss and Ivy. And off they went with Santa and Mrs. Claws.

They saw the doll factory...

the bicycle works...

the sled shop...

and the ice-skate testing rink.
"Oh, boy!" exclaimed Peat
Moss and Ivy. "Are we getting
new ice skates like those?"
"Of course!" said Santa.
"Isn't that what you asked
for?"

But then Ivy remembered—
Hickory Gray Squirrel wanted
new ice skates too!

"Do you think Hickory will
get what he wants for Christmas?"
she whispered to her brother.

"I guess not." Peat Moss shrugged.
"He didn't tell Santa Claws."

"Come along now!" said Santa.
"It's time to inspect the stables."

In the stables, Peat Moss and Ivy fed
carrots to the snowshoe hares who pulled
Santa's sleigh. Mrs. Claws dusted off
the sleigh. Santa oiled the runners.

"You know, Claws," said his wife, "these children are a long way from home and it's getting late."

"Don't worry, my dear," said Santa. "I'll take them home. It's time I took these bunnies out for a practice run, anyway. We have to get ready for the big night, you know."

Santa Claws put on his big red coat. He hitched the hares to the sleigh and climbed aboard. Peat Moss and Ivy hopped in behind him.

Mrs. Claws opened two big doors to the outside. Santa gave the reins a shake, and with a "ho ho ho" and a "giddy-yap" they were off. Away they went— down Snow Mountain, over the hills, around the pond, through the woods, toward the People House…and Peat Moss and Ivy's own backyard.

Santa pulled up just beyond
the backyard fence.

"Thanks, Santa!" cried Peat
Moss and Ivy, climbing down.
"See you on Christmas Eve."

"If you can stay awake," said Santa, laughing.
"And, by the way, I wouldn't worry about
that friend of yours, Hickory Gray Squirrel—
he'll get his new ice skates!"

"New ice skates!" cried Peat Moss and Ivy.
"How did *you* know about that?"

"It wasn't too hard to figure out," Santa said. "Hickory told me himself." He pulled a letter out of his pocket and showed it to the chipmunks.

Dear Santa Claws,
Could you please bring me a new pair of ice skates, please? Thanks.
Your Friend,
Hickory Gray Squirrel
P.S. Can I have a new hockey stick, too?   H.G.S.

"Then Hickory believes in you after all!" said Peat Moss.

"Yes!" said Ivy. "But why did he say that he *didn't?*"

"Maybe he thought it would sound smart," said Santa. "Some folks think it sounds smart not to believe in things." And with a wave and a chuckle he was off—on his way back to Snow Mountain. "So long!" he called. "Merry Christmas!"

As Peat Moss and Ivy walked home they thought about their exciting day. They could hardly wait until Christmas!

On Christmas morning the Chipmunk family gathered in front of the Christmas twig to open their presents. Poppa got a new tie and slippers. Momma got a red kerchief and a holly berry necklace. Peat Moss and Ivy got some books and some toys—and shiny new ice skates!

"Just like Santa promised!" said Ivy.

Then there was a loud knock at the front hole, and in came Hickory Gray Squirrel.

"Look!" he said, proudly holding up a new pair of ice skates. "See what Santa Claws brought me!"

"*Santa Claws?*" said Peat Moss and Ivy, smiling at each other. "We thought you didn't believe in him!"

"Oh, yeah," said Hickory quickly. "I mean, look what my mom and pop gave me."

"Great!" said Peat Moss. "We got new skates too. Let's go try 'em out."

"Yes, Hickory," agreed Ivy. "And why don't you bring along your *new hockey stick*, too?"

"Okay," said Hickory. "I left it outside....Hey! How did you know about my new hockey stick?"

"Oh, never mind," said Ivy as the three friends headed down to the skating pond. "If I told you, you probably wouldn't believe in it anyway!"